Grandma Stories

An imprint of Om Books International

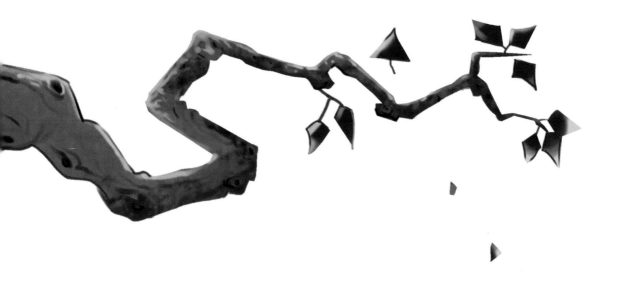

 Om **Books International**

Reprinted in 2020

Corporate & Editorial Office
A-12, Sector 64, Noida 201 301
Uttar Pradesh, India
Phone: +91 120 477 4100
Email: editorial@ombooks.com
Website: www.ombooksinternational.com

Sales Office
107, Ansari Road, Darya Ganj
New Delhi 110 002, India
Phone: +91 11 4000 9000
Email: sales@ombooks.com
Website: www.ombooks.com

ISBN : 978-93-81607-44-2

Printed in India

10 9 8 7 6 5 4

Contents

The Red Dots

It was a hot, sunny afternoon. Lizzy, Teddy and Alex had no choice but to stay indoors. They had planned a picnic at the lake, but here they were, watching the sleepy afternoon from their playroom window.

6

When Grandma came into the room, Alex complained to her, "There is nothing to do today, Grandma. How long can we just play inside the house!"

"Is that all?" said Grandma, sitting down in her rocking chair. "Would you kids like to listen to a story then?"

The children all gathered around Grandma and sat down by her feet. "Sure, Grandma! What story are you going to tell us today?"

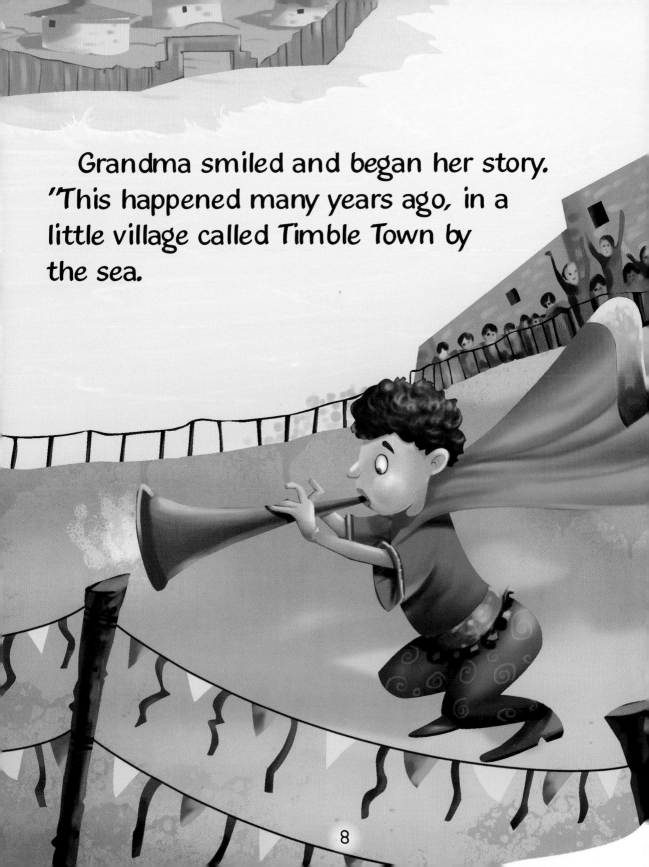

Grandma smiled and began her story. "This happened many years ago, in a little village called Timble Town by the sea.

"The big
St. Patrick's Day
parade was taking
place in the city, a little
away from the village.
All the adults had gone to the
city to take part in the festival.

9

"They left a young girl, Lithia, in charge of the children. After all, someone had to stay behind and take care of them, for they were too young to go. Young Lithia and the children were very fond of each other.

"Lithia asked the children to go and play, as she sat down to catch up on her knitting. The children were having fun, building sandcastles and playing fetch on the beach, when suddenly someone screamed rather loudly.

Lithia looked up to see a man waving and running in her direction. 'Run, run, run,' the man screamed, 'The pirates are coming. Save yourself while you can.' And so saying, the man ran away.

"Lithia could not just run away. She had to make sure that the children were safe first. She also knew that she couldn't just run with the children. They would surely get captured by the pirates.

"So she decided to outsmart the pirates in order to save the children of the village and herself.

"She called the children and told them what they had to do. Once the children were ready, Lithia started moving towards the beach, to meet the terrifying pirates!

"As soon as the pirates saw her, they came charging towards her. The chief of the pirates asked her, 'Why is the village so quiet? Where is everybody?'

"Lithia started breathing very heavily and replied, 'Oh, thank goodness you are here! The

children are all suffering from a very weird disease, and the elders have all gone to the city. I don't know what to do! Help us!' Just then, as per Lithia's plan, Tommy came to her, walking weakly, his face covered with all sorts of red dots.

"The pirate Chief was a little alarmed on seeing the state Tommy was in. 'Aaah!' he exclaimed, 'All the children have this disease?' Lithia nodded her head and replied, 'Yes... it started with one child and then all the other children caught it. It is highly infectious...'

"Even before Lithia could complete what she had started to say, the pirate chief yelled to his men, 'Come on, move, run, escape! We have landed at the wrong place. Run, before we all have these red dots on our faces!'

"Within the next few seconds, the pirates were back up on their ship and had almost sailed back to the horizon. Lithia had managed to save all the children from harm's way."

As Grandma finished telling this story, Lizzy asked her, "Granny, isn't this story about you? Aren't you Lithia?"

Grandma flashed a large smile towards the children. She was too embarrassed to agree that she was indeed Lithia.

The Talking Objects

Lizzy was a very naughty and untidy girl.
Her room always had things thrown about
here and there—clothes and toys on the floor,
books and pencils off the desk!

However much Lizzy's parents or teachers
tried explaining to her, she would just not
learn. She treated everything around her with
complete disregard and disrespect.

Seeing her mother always grumbling about Lizzy's attitude, her grandma decided to see if she could help Lizzy understand the value of her belongings.

One Friday, as Lizzy came back from school, she threw her shoes off and then dumped her bag on the couch. Grandma came into the room and saw it all. Sighing and sitting down on the couch, she asked Lizzy, "Would you like to hear a story, my child?"

Lizzy loved Grandma's stories and in a flash she sat down before the sofa, smiling eagerly up at Grandma.

"This is the story of a boy named Robin," Grandma began, "and what happened to him one fine morning. Till date he does not know how it happened, but he agrees that it did change his life!

"Robin treated everything around him very shabbily. That morning when the alarm clock rang, Robin was about to crash his fist through the clock as usual. But just as he raised his hand, the clock screamed, 'Oh no, not today! Why do you keep punching me like this every morning?'

"Robin jolted out of his sleep. His alarm clock had just spoken to him! How on earth could that have happened? Robin was really spooked and turned off the alarm with a gentle click.

"He then went to brush his teeth. But just as he was about to grab his toothpaste, the tube warned him, 'Stop squeezing me so hard every morning. You needn't kill me everyday, you know!'

"And again, as he reached for his
toothbrush, the brush said, 'Be gentle with
me! I clean your teeth, I don't break them!'

"All the objects that he used in his daily life were giving Robin all kinds of advice. The school bag spoke to him too, saying, 'You can at least pack your umbrella and racket in another bag. What have I ever done to deserve this?'

"Robin understood what was happening. He had treated all his things very poorly and they were all speaking up now.

"At school, Robin's mathematics teacher asked him to solve a problem on the board. Now, the chalk that he had in his hands screeched, 'Yesterday, you were rubbing my friends against the board and finishing them uselessly. Just wait and watch what I do to you now!' And so Robin's 2+2 equalled to a duck!

"That's how Robin learnt his lesson. He was careful with all his belongings after that day. He took good care of them so that they never had a reason to complain again."

As Grandma completed her story, Lizzy said, "Grandma, Robin was a very rude boy. It was a good thing that happened to him."

Grandma smiled and replied, "And one day, dear Lizzy, your belongings will talk to you too if you don't treat them gently."

Lizzy realised what her Grandma was telling her. Since then, Lizzy never gave her belongings a chance to complain.

Little Red Riding Hood

Joyce came to see Grandma when she was ill. She brought with her a delicious cake and fruits. Grandma was very happy.

"Let me tell you a story about a little girl who loved her Grandma very much," her grandma said.

"This little girl was called Red Riding Hood, and she always looked for excuses to go visit her grandma, who lived on the other side of the woods.

"One day, when Red Riding Hood learnt that Grandma was ill, she decided to pay her a visit. Red Riding Hood set off early in the morning, her basket full of goodies for her dear grandmother.

"Just as she was about to reach her grandmother's house, a wolf saw Red Riding Hood making haste through the woods. The hungry wolf decided to make a meal out of her. Hoping to find out where she was headed, he went up to Red Riding Hood.

"'Hello! Where
are you off to, so
early in the morning?'
he asked.

"'I am going to see my
grandmother... She lives right down
the path, in the log cabin,' replied
little Red Riding Hood.

'Oh! then you must pluck some of these pretty flowers for your dear granny!' Saying that the wolf sent of Red Riding Hood to pluck some wild flowers.

"He then rushed off straight for her grandmother's house and climbed in through the window. He hid the grandmother in the closet and jumped into her bed, putting on her cap and robe!

"Soon, Red Riding Hood arrived with a bunch of pretty flowers in her hand. But when she saw her grandmother, she felt that she looked quite different from last time.

"Red Riding Hood said to the disguised wolf, 'My, what big hands you have, Grandmum!'

'All the better to hold you, my dear,' said the wolf.

"Red Riding Hood then exclaimed, 'My, what big eyes you have, Grandmum!'

'All the better to see you with, my child!' said the wolf with a sugary sweet smile.

"But right then, Red Riding Hood screamed, 'Goodness, what large teeth you have, Grandmother!'

"And without wasting another moment, the wolf sprung towards Red Riding Hood, screaming, 'All the better to eat you with!'

"Red Riding Hood ran around the cabin, shouting for help. Luckily, a hunter was travelling through the forest. Hearing the little girl's screams for help, he ran into the cabin and knocked the wolf out with a swing of his stick.

"Red Riding Hood breathed a sigh of relief as the wolf was carried away from there. Her grandmother had been released from the closet, all safe and sound."

As Grandma finished her story, Lizzy, Teddy, Alex and Joyce clapped with joy. Red Riding Hood had to go through such trouble to visit her grandmother. Thankfully, it was much easier for Joyce.

Pinocchio

One day, Teddy's mother complained to Grandma, "You know, I think Teddy is starting to lie. Yesterday, he told me that he had gone to school. But I met Mrs Auburn, Teddy's class teacher, in the market today, and she says that Teddy was not in class! I am worried about him!"

That evening, as Teddy came back from school, Grandma asked him, "So dear, how was school today?"

Teddy didn't quite look at Grandma, but replied, "It was the usual, Grandma!"

Grandma knew that Teddy had not gone to school that day as well. She therefore replied, "Ah! But Teddy, your nose is growing!"

"What do you mean, Grandma? How can my nose grow?" exclaimed Teddy, taken aback by what Grandma was saying.

Now it was Grandma's turn to be surprised. "What? Haven't you heard about Pinocchio?" she asked. Teddy could only shake his head. Without wasting another moment, Grandma sat down and was all ready to tell Teddy the story of the puppet who lied.

"Geppetto, a poor old wood carver, started work on making a puppet from a piece of wood. As he carefully carved through the wood, he remarked, You shall be my little boy. What he did not expect, though, was the puppet to say, 'Hello, there!' as soon as Geppetto was finished with it.

"Needless to say, Geppetto was extremely surprised. He had not expected a puppet made of wood to speak. 'How on earth did you do that?' asked a bewildered Geppetto.

"The puppet had more to say to that. You gave me a mouth and therefore I can

speak. How is that so difficult to understand?' said the puppet. 'Here,' continued the wooden boy, 'I can do a lot more than just talk.' And so saying, it started to dance, throwing its hands and legs in the air.

"Geppetto was indeed very impressed with his creation. He named the puppet Pinocchio and decided that Pinocchio would go to school and learn with all the normal children.

"The next day, Pinocchio waved goodbye to Geppetto as he left for school. However,

even before he could get there, Pinocchio stopped to see a puppet show which was in progress in the park

"As Pinocchio saw a couple of shows, he thought to himself, 'Hmmm! I can not only sing and dance better than those puppets, I don't even need those ugly looking strings.'

"And so, Pinocchio forgot all about school and jumped on to the stage and started to dance and sing. The puppet master realised that people liked Pinocchio's show, so he did not say anything then.

"But as soon as the show was over, he caught Pinocchio by his nose and threw him off the stage, warning him, 'Don't ever come back here. You're just a puppet, not a real boy!'

"Pinocchio was naturally very upset. He sobbed and sobbed. What does the puppet master think of himself? I am just like a real boy!' Pinocchio reasoned with himself.

"Suddenly, Pinocchio saw a pink fairy come before him. Who are you?' asked a surprised Pinocchio.

"The fairy smiled and replied, 'I am your Guardian Fairy, Pinocchio. I saw you crying and so I came to pay you a visit. How was school today?'

"Pinocchio kept a straight face and said, 'School was fun. I learnt quite a lot today.'

"No sooner did Pinocchio say this, his nose jumped up and grew a little longer. Pinocchio tried pressing on his nose, but it just did not go back in. He looked with surprise at his Guardian Fairy.

"What is happening? Why is my nose growing like this?" asked a surprised Pinocchio. But his Guardian Fairy merely replied, 'Every time you tell a lie, dear Pinocchio, your nose will grow like this. And every time you speak the truth, it will go back inside the same distance.'

"But Pinocchio was adamant. 'I did not lie even once. I did indeed go to school,' cried the little puppet boy. And even as he finished speaking, his nose grew longer.

"Pinocchio's Guardian Fairy then said, 'It is better if you stop lying. Now go home and remember, you will turn into a real boy only

if you are brave and honest. So never tell lies again and always try to be honest and brave.' So saying, his Guardian Fairy left.

"Pinocchio decided to go back home to Geppetto. But as he was walking past the beach, he saw the same puppet master walking along the sea shore. Seeing Pinocchio

walk towards him again, the angry puppet master grabbed his head, and threw the poor puppet into the sea.

"Even before Pinocchio knew what was happening, a giant whale came and gobbled him up. As Pinocchio landed in the whale's belly, he felt someone's breath on him.

"Who are you?" screamed Pinocchio.

"Pinocchio, is that you?" asked the other person in return. It was Geppetto! He had been looking for Pinocchio when he didn't return from school, and was washed to sea by a big wave and then swallowed by a whale.

"Pinocchio ran into Geppetto's arms, 'I am so sorry, I lied to you. I'll never lie again!' Pinocchio was not scared any more. He then helped Geppetto make a raft strong enough to carry them both.

'"Father, I will tickle the whale from inside his mouth, get ready to leave the moment he sneezes,' said Pinocchio.

"And lo and behold, both Geppetto and Pinocchio were soon on their way home as soon as the whale sneezed. That night as

Geppetto tucked Pinocchio in his bed, he said, 'You are my son, and I shall always love you. Today you have been brave, and honest, Pinocchio and I hope you grow up just like this.'

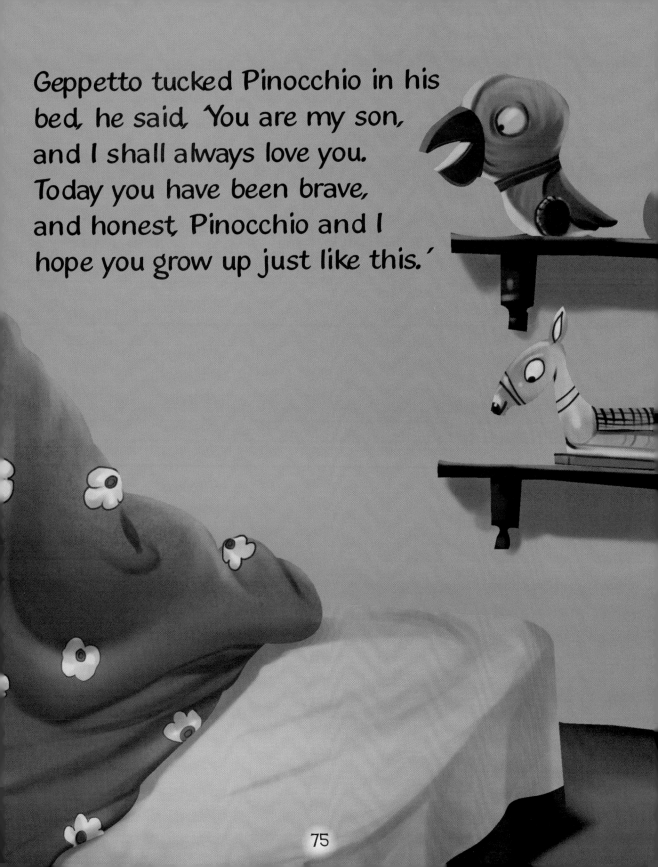

"Pinocchio remembered what his Guardian Fairy had said to him. As he drifted off to sleep, Pinocchio wondered whether her words would at all come true.

"Next morning, as Geppetto got out of bed, he saw Pinocchio come running towards him, yelling. 'Look father, I am a real boy!'"

As she finished her tale, Grandma looked at Teddy once again and said, "So, my dear little Teddy, how was school today?"

Teddy looked down towards the floor, as he replied, "Grandma, I don't want my nose to grow like Pinocchio, so I'll tell you the truth. I went to the circus with my friends, I didn't go to school."

"But," Teddy continued, "I will never ever lie again. And I will also make sure that I do indeed go to school from now on. I have learnt my lesson."

Grandma was very pleased to hear Teddy admit his mistake. She winked at Teddy, letting him know that this was just going to be their little secret.

OTHER TITLES IN THIS SERIES